Dear Parent:

Congratulations! Your child is taking the first steps on an exciting journey. The destination? Independent reading!

STEP INTO READING® will help your child get there. The program offers books at five levels that accompany children from their first attempts at reading to reading success. Each step includes fun stories, fiction and nonfiction, and colorful art. There are also Step into Reading Sticker Books, Step into Reading Math Readers, and Step into Reading Phonics Readers— a complete literacy program with something to interest every child.

Learning to Read, Step by Step!

Ready to Read Preschool–Kindergarten
• big type and easy words • rhyme and rhythm • picture clues
For children who know the alphabet and are eager to begin reading.

Reading with Help Preschool–Grade 1
• basic vocabulary • short sentences • simple stories
For children who recognize familiar words and sound out new words with help.

Reading on Your Own Grades 1–3
• engaging characters • easy-to-follow plots • popular topics
For children who are ready to read on their own.

Reading Paragraphs Grades 2–3
• challenging vocabulary • short paragraphs • exciting stories
For newly independent readers who read simple sentences with confidence.

Ready for Chapters Grades 2–4
• chapters • longer paragraphs • full-color art
For children who want to take the plunge into chapter books but still like colorful pictures.

STEP INTO READING® is designed to give every child a successful reading experience. The grade levels are only guides. Children can progress through the steps at their own speed, developing confidence in their reading, no matter what their grade.

Remember, a lifetime love of reading starts with a single step!

For my mom and dad
—K.C.

For Samantha
—A.C.

Text copyright © 1992 by Kathryn Cristaldi. Illustrations copyright © 1992 by Abby Carter. All rights reserved under International and Pan-American Copyright Conventions. Published in the United States by Random House Children's Books, a division of Random House, Inc., New York, and simultaneously in Canada by Random House of Canada Limited, Toronto.

www.stepintoreading.com

Educators and librarians, for a variety of teaching tools, visit us at www.randomhouse.com/teachers

Library of Congress Cataloging-in-Publication Data
Cristaldi, Kathryn.
Baseball ballerina / by Kathryn Cristaldi ; illustrated by Abby Carter.
    p.   cm. — (Step into reading. A step 3 book)
SUMMARY: A baseball-loving girl worries that the ballet class her mother forces her to take will ruin her reputation with the other members of her baseball team.
ISBN 0-679-81734-4 (trade) — ISBN 0-679-91734-9 (lib. bdg.)
[1. Ballet dancing—Fiction.   2. Sex role—Fiction.   3. Baseball—Fiction.]
I. Carter, Abby, ill.   II. Title   III. Series: Step into reading. Step 3 book.
PZ7.C86964 Bas 2003 [E]—dc21 2002013215

Printed in the United States of America   42 41 40 39 38 37 36 35 34 33

STEP INTO READING, RANDOM HOUSE, and the Random House colophon are registered trademarks of Random House, Inc.

STEP INTO READING®

STEP 3

Baseball Ballerina

By Kathryn Cristaldi

Illustrated by Abby Carter

Random House New York

Chapter 1:

BALLET LESSONS

I love to play ball.

I play shortstop on a team

called the Sharks.

We wear neat hats

and cool green T-shirts.

Mom thinks baseball
is for boys.
She wants me to do
more girl things.

6

That is how I got stuck

taking ballet lessons.

I have pink tights
and pink slippers.
Mom puts a pink ribbon
in my hair.
She says, "Pink is for girls."
I hate pink.

In class I sit next to
my best friend, Mary Ann.
She is the catcher
for the Sharks.
Her mother made her
take ballet too.

Mary Ann and I have a deal.

We must keep ballet a secret.

If the other Sharks found out,

they would laugh.

They would think

we were wimps.

Madame is our teacher.
She is very old
and very strict.

Mary Ann said she saw
her smile once.
I must have blinked,
because I missed it.

Every class starts the same.

First we line up at the barre.

Then we practice the five positions.

First position.

Second position.

Third position.

I make a face.

There is only one position for me.

Shortstop.

Sometimes I pretend

I am up at bat.

Madame is our coach.

"Heels on the floor!

Shoulders back!

Point the toes!"

she shouts.

Who knows?

Maybe pointy toes

will help my swing.

Madame loves flowers.

Last week we were buttercups.

This week we are dandelions.

"Pretend you are a dandelion

swaying in the wind," she says.

She waves her arms.

"Look, I'm stuck in a tornado,"
Mary Ann whispers.
She spins around and around
really fast.
I giggle.

Madame walks over to Mary Ann.

My friend is in trouble now!

But our teacher <u>smiles</u>.

"Very lively, my dear!"

she says.

Chapter 2:

RECITAL BLUES

One day after class
Madame has some news.
"In two weeks
there will be a recital.
You will get to dance
on a big stage."

I feel like I just

got hit with a line drive.

I do not want to dance

on a big stage.

I do not want to dance

on any stage.

What if someone sees me?

What if the <u>Sharks</u> see me?

They will think I like
girl stuff.

They will not want

a ballerina for a shortstop.

Madame puts her arm

around Mary Ann.

She tells the class,

"You will be doing

The Dance of the Dandelions.

Mary Ann will be Queen Dandelion."

Everyone claps.

They pat my friend on the back.

"Too bad," I say to Mary Ann.

But she looks happy.

"I wonder if I get to

wear a crown?" she says.

For the next two weeks

we get ready for the big night.

It is worse than I thought.

We have to wear green tights
with lace on them.
We have to wear big,
fluffy hats.

I flap my leaves at Mary Ann.

"Look at me," I say.

"I'm wilting!"

But she does not laugh.

Something strange is
happening to my friend.
It started when Madame
chose her to be Queen Dandelion.
She <u>does</u> get to wear a special crown.
Sometimes she even
wears it home!

Chapter 3:

THE BIG NIGHT

It is the big night.

I am nervous.

I peek out from

behind the curtain.

I see my mother

and my baby sister.

Strike one!

I see my uncle Ethan

and my aunt Agnes.

Strike two!!

And then I see them.

They are sitting

in the third row.

They are wearing neat hats

and cool green T-shirts.

It is the Sharks!

Strike three!!!

"The Sharks are out there,"

I tell Mary Ann.

"They will laugh at us.

They will think

we are wimps."

But my friend just smiles.

"I hope they will like my crown,"

she says.

40

I feel sick.

But Madame says,

"The show must go on."

I close my eyes.

I pretend I am about

to play in the World Series.

I am still nervous.

But I cannot let the team down.

I do not think about

the Sharks.

Tonight my team is called

the Dandelions.

The curtain goes up.

Heels on the floor!

Shoulders back!

Point the toes!

Now it is time for

Queen Dandelion.

Mary Ann leaps on stage.

Suddenly her crown flies

off her head.

Up, up, up it goes!

It is a high pop.

The crowd gasps.

I dance across the stage.

I make the catch.

Everyone cheers.

Mary Ann giggles.

Afterward, the Sharks

give me high fives.

"You were great!" they say.

I feel like I just hit a home run.

Maybe ballet isn't

so bad after all.

But I still like baseball best!